TOO MANY LATKES!

To Betsy and Hai Knaffo,
who never tire of Too Many Latkes

Other books by Richard Codor:

Richard Codor's Joyous Haggadah
www.joyoushaggadah.com

and

All You Want to Know
About Sabbath Services, A Guide for the Perplexed
written by Rabbi Samuel Barth
Published by Behrman House

Art direction and design by Liora Codor
Too Many Latkes! by Richard Codor

Published by Behrman House, Inc.
Copyright © 2011
Springfield, NJ 07081
www.behrmanhouse.com

TOO MANY LATKES!

Written and illustrated by

Richard Codor

Behrman House Publishers
www.behrmanhouse.com

Once upon a time, there was a little house nestled right in the heart of the big city. It was a friendly little house, even though it needed some care and fixing up.

The name of the family that lived in the slightly run-down house was Smalls: Dad, Mom, Tamara and Ronen Smalls. They were a happy, small family, but they needed some fixing up, too.

Dad worked for the Tip Top Pencil Company. He was their Eraser Supervisor. It was precise work and often he stayed late at the workshop. However, tonight was different and he left early. He had to buy decorations, food and presents because tonight was the first night of Hanukkah.

Unfortunately, there was one thing that Dad forgot.

He wasn't paid that day. He was broke.

As poor, miserable Dad wondered what to do, a strange little man walked up to him.

"Excuse me my friend, you look very unhappy. Nobody should be unhappy on the first night of Hanukkah," he said.

"I barely have money to get home, let alone buy anything for our celebration," Dad replied.

"I think I have something that will cheer you up." And as the strange little man proceeded to rummage around in his beaten-up old briefcase, he cheerfully announced, "This is a present I've waited a long time to give. Only the most deserving person will recognize its true worth. Only that special person can find in it the true magic of Hanukkah. Here, for you my friend, the unique and wonderful..."

...Potato!

With a wink and a smile, the little man handed Dad his present.
"Magic? Unique? Wait, I don't understand..." but the little man
was gone.

Dad looked at the potato and wondered, "Can it grant wishes?
Tell fortunes? Sing? Dance?" The potato didn't do anything.

"Well, maybe it's just shy."

So Dad made his way home worrying how he was going to explain the magic potato to the family.

He was happily greeted as he walked through the door.

"Bring in the groceries, dear," said Mom.

"Let's hang the decorations," said Tamara.

"Lights!" said Ronen.

"Oh boy, do I have a surprise for you," said Dad.

"TA-DA!"

Dad put the potato on the dining room table.

"Isn't it great!" he said. "It looks like an ordinary potato, but the strange little man who gave it to me said it's a special, magic Hanukkah potato."

"What does it do?" asked Ronen.

"I don't know," said Dad.

"You shouldn't take presents from strangers," said Tamara.

"Next time maybe he could also spare an onion," said Mom.

Mom took the potato to the kitchen. Following her traditional recipe, she peeled it, sliced it, diced it, chopped it, added an egg, this spice, that spice, a little bit of salt, a little bit of pepper, a little bit of flour, and before long she had one small potato latke.

She put it in a big frying pan, covered it, turned on the fire and left the latke to fry.

In the dining room they lit the first candle, said the blessings and sang the old songs. Things weren't really as bad as they seemed. It was still the joyous Festival of Lights.

Until Mom noticed that something was burning!

Mom ran back into the kitchen and pulled the smoking pan off the stove.

When she lifted the lid she was sure there would be one burnt, shriveled potato pancake. Instead, there were five big, juicy, hot latkes!

"How did that happen?" exclaimed Mom.

"You're a great cook," Dad said, and they all agreed.

They sat down to their grand latke dinner and it was very tasty.
"There's one latke left," said Tamara. "Who is going to get it?"

"Let's save it," Mom replied, looking at Dad. "Who knows, we
may need it tomorrow."

She covered up the frying pan, put it on the kitchen table,
turned off the lights and then they all went to bed.

When everything was dark and quiet in the house, something strange started to happen to the frying pan. It started to quake and shake.

Meantime, Dad dreamt of a wondrous bakeshop where Mom cooked scrumptious latkes. She made latkes covered in applesauce, pineapple sauce, topped with raisins, cherries and blueberries. They looked so good he could almost taste them. He could almost smell them.

Then Dad woke up.

"They're real! They're on the bed! They're all over the room! Honey, get up. Look!"

"Oh leave me alone. I was having such a nice dream," said Mom sleepily. "What's that? Oh my goodness!"

They jumped out of bed and ran into the hall. At least they tried to run into the hall, but running through latkes is like running through thick, mushy, hot...latkes.

"They're everywhere," screamed Dad.

"Quick, the kitchen," yelled Mom.

When they made their way to the kitchen, they couldn't believe their eyes. Latkes were jumping out of the frying pan too fast to count. Big ones, fat ones, small ones, tall ones. They watched in amazement as latkes flew from the frying pan.

"Wake up the kids," cried Mom.

They struggled through the hall to the children's room but the door was jammed shut. They pushed and pushed until it finally opened. Mom and Dad tried to reach them, but, the latkes swelled under the children's beds like a huge wave and carried them like a surfboard out of the window.

"Tamara! Ronen! Wake up!" Mom and Dad shouted, but the children were fast asleep and didn't hear a thing.

Mom and Dad ran outside. They yelled and yelled, but the children slept on. They watched helplessly as the growing latke pile lifted the beds straight up into the sky.

Dad tried to climb up the slippery latke slope, but slid back down. The neighbors, awakened by all the commotion, quickly brought ladders, ropes and chairs. But, nothing helped. They couldn't reach the sleeping Ronen and Tamara. The latke mountain just grew and grew.

Someone called 911, and soon police cars, fire engines and ambulances were rushing from all over the city to the Smalls' house.

"All right," said the Police Chief, "everybody stand back. We'll take over."

The brave fireman raised the tallest ladder and climbed to its top, but the latke mountain grew faster and faster out of reach.

"It's no use," said the fireman.
"We need reinforcements," said the Police Chief.

Soon a police helicopter arrived, but every time the helicopter tried to get near and throw a rescue line, the latke mountain would wobble and wiggle and slip away.

All they could do was watch as the mountain grew higher and higher.

"Isn't there anybody who can help us?" cried Mom. "Isn't there someone who knows what to do?"

Then, right in front of them, out of the noisy crowd and the flashing lights, the little old man appeared.

"It's him! He's the one who gave me the potato!" said Dad.

Everyone gathered around as Dad talked to the little old man.

"Look what happened! You told me your gift held the true meaning of Hanukkah and we made it into latkes and went to sleep and it grew into this monstrous mountain and took my children away. Please, you must save them."

The crowd grew very quiet as the little old man listened silently to Dad and thoughtfully stroked his beard. Then his face lit up with a big toothy smile and he said...

"LET'S EAT!"

"Dig in everybody!" said Dad. "Everybody in town is invited!"
Then the police officers, the firefighters, the ambulance crew,
the rescue squad, the news people, and the neighbors all grabbed
a latke.

They all called their friends and relatives and more and more people came as word of an all-you-can-eat latke party spread throughout the city.

At first, nothing seemed to happen, then slowly, slowly and faster and faster the latke mountain shrank.

Soon, it wasn't a mountain anymore, or a hill, or even a little pile.

Before long, all the latkes were gone.

When the beds landed with a gentle bump on the ground the children rubbed their eyes and looked around.

"Mom, Dad, what are we doing outside? Who are all these people and what is that delicious smell?"

Meantime, the little old man walked among the crowd saying, "You ate well and had a good time, yes? You know these nice people are going to have a big cleanup bill. How about showing your appreciation with a little Hanukkah gelt for the holiday?"

People threw in a few pennies here and few pennies there and soon the bag was full.

The little old man gave the overflowing bag to the Smalls and said, "Now here is a present you can really use."

Afterwards, Dad quit his job and the Smalls turned their house into a real bakery. They made every kind of cookie, cake and bread. People bought everything and their small business did very well.

However, there was one thing they never sold...

LATKES!